SPECIAL

By SALEEM LITTLE

MITANNI PUBLISHING LLC
Copyright ©2019 by Saleem Little
Produced by SALEEM LITTLE

SPECIAL

The Prologue

Sophia: He read me poems while he talked spiritedly about the life in him that had awakened since meeting me. Staring me in my eyes he read the words...

"She's in the house
She's at turn after turn
She's behind me
She's in front of me
She's in my bed
She's on path after path
And I'm weak from want of her,
O heart,
There is no reality for me
Other than she, she, she, she..."

"I swear I could sue him for plagiarism Sophia." He had said to me so playfully. I loved him, he was so misunderstood. And the fact that I understood him was my key, it was my personal key to his heart. I became his new existence; I was his breath of life, the only color in his black and white world.

"You're ruling the way I move, and I breathe your air..."

Sade had sung to him and her romantic sonnets became the ambitions of his inner romantic. His dream woman would personify the lyrics to his favorite Sade songs...I was the embodiment of those lyrics to him.

We fought once. I said. *"You don't really know me."*

He said. *"I beg to differ."*

I said. *"Why is that?"*

He said. *"To say I don't know you is to say I don't know myself. We're one in the same."*

"How do you figure?" I asked.

"How do you figure we're not?" he shot right back.

Not in the mood to play his game I said, *"I have a past."*

He simply said,

"And so do I. Every rose has its thorns, and he who wants a rose must respect the thorns. One of the most admired flowers can also be one of the most painful...like love..."

Dante was deep. I always wondered if she knew that side of him. O well, I did, and that's all that really mattered. We would have run away together, I know it, but she took him away from me before I could tell him that he too had brought me back to life.

Lena: This man was my world. I couldn't imagine a life without Dante? What had I done? Why had I decided to play such a stupid game? I could never imagine sharing my fiancé with anoth'... what was I thinking? This man had introduced me to so much in life. He'd broadened my perspective in so many areas and now... here... he... because of... me...here he...lay... His chest heaved...and then...it stopped. His last breath, warm but chilled by death and fogged by the mixture, blew slowly onto my face after I shot him. *"Lena"*, he cried... *"I'm sorry"* he pleaded. And then...he was no more. That scent... mortification... it would stain the fibers of my brain and the hairs of my nose and I would smell the death of Dante forever...My eternal punishment for taking the life of the man I loved... forgive me...

Curiosity

Dante shot a quizzical look at Lena. This had to be a setup. There was no way she was asking him this with no ulterior motive or hidden agenda. She had to be asking merely to gauge his response. Dante knew he had to be very careful with his response.

"Listen Lena, if this is one of your little test to see how much I love you..."

"No, no..." Lena interrupted.

"I promise it's not a test. I really wanted to know. I've been thinking about it for a while now. I was actually hoping you wouldn't get mad at me for suggesting it."

"Mad at you?" Dante thought. He had actually been thrilled by the idea. Like most men, and women for that matter, he had long given thought to what a threesome would be like and in his twenty-seven years had yet to experience one. To have two women at once was probably at the top of any man's list of fantasies. Considering suggesting it may have been seen as a sign of mental infidelity, he had never built up the courage to ask. Dante had always been very committed to his relationship with Lena but was very much interested in her idea. No matter how interested however, he reminded himself to maintain his composure and conceal any excitement.

"I mean, you know, if that's something *you* want to do, if it would make *you* happy...I guess I would be cool with it."

Lena smiled.

"Stop it Dante, you know you've thought about it before."

"Maybe once or twice..." Dante said smiling. He could see that Lena was onto his game.

"Yea right, I bet more than twice."

"You're probably right, maybe three times." Dante teased.

Lena shook her head and playfully rolled her eyes at him.

"Ok, you're right, so I have thought about it before, quite a few times, what man hasn't?"

"Have you done it before?" Lena asked, her expression turning serious.

"No."

"Don't lie to me Dante. It's not like I'll be mad."

"*It's not like I'll be mad...*Why do women say that knowing that if what they hear is not what they *want* to hear they *will* get mad?"

"Just answer the question."

"I did, I said no. I've thought about it before, yes, but I've never actually gone through with the act before."

"Ok, I believe you." Lena said.

"So this would be a new experience for both of us then?" She asked still seeking a little more confirmation that Dante hadn't done this before.

"Yup...cross my heart, hope to die." Dante smiled and finally, Lena did as well.

There was silence as they both began to imagine what the experience would be like. Dante hoped the other woman would be just as beautiful as Lena and Lena hoped the same.

Dante glanced over at the *King* magazine Lena had been reading and felt the need to internally thank the vixen on the cover: Nicki Minaj. Obviously the idea had been prompted by her reading of Nicki Minaj's article. The thought may had surfaced a long time ago, it's not unusual for women to be attracted to the beauty of other women, but the trending nature of bisexuality was making more women comfortable with admitting their curiosity and more so, acting on it.

Lena broke the silence.

"So it's settled then, we're definitely gonna try this?" She now seemed to be just as excited as Dante was pretending not to be.

"Guess so…"

"Well, I think we need to lay down some rules."

"Laws for a lawless act…" Dante said sarcastically under his breath.

"What did you say?"

"Nothing."

"What did you say Dante?"

"Nothing baby, what are the rules?"

"Whatever…Ok, listen, she has to be clean."

"Well that goes without saying."

"She has to be pretty."

"Ummm…I think that's an unwritten rule luv." Dante said, unable to contain his laughter.

"Give me a break, I didn't plan this weeks ago, I'm coming up with these as I go." Lena said.

"Ok, I gotchu…next rule?"

"This is a one-night thing. We do it then we walk away. I don't care how much we like it, it never happens again."

"Fair enough."

"I'm serious Dante. I'm sure you'll like it even more than me but once it's done it's done!"

"Ok   Lena."

"I get to pick the girl."

"What? Wait, why do you get to pick the girl?"

"Because I have to be comfortable with the situation. You're a man, you'll be fine with anything and I might not like your taste."

"Wait, what's wrong with my taste? I picked you, didn't I?"

"We picked each other."

"Yea, well *we* can pick this girl together too."

"Ok, whatever...hmmm, I'm scared to see what you would have been with if you weren't with me."

"What?" Dante said unable to make out the last part of Lena's mumbled sentence.

"Nothing. Moving on...I'm not going down on her."

Dante smiled.

"I thought that was part of it but, ok, whatever."

"You're not either."

"C'mon Lena. Why are you trying to put so many limitations on this thing? Next you'll say don't kiss her; maybe don't look at her and the lights have to be off. If that's the case we might as well not even go through with it. Look, it's one night of fun. One night where we let go of all the rules, all inhibitions and just have fun. The point is this is for *one* night, so why not go all out that *one* night and enjoy ourselves unencumbered by rules and limitations?"

"Well, I'll...*we'll* just go with the flow and see what happens I guess."

"Now that's more like it."

"Wait. One more thing..."

Dante rolled his eyes.

"You're never to see or speak to this woman ever again after this is over."

"You said that already Lena. Relax. It's just an experiment. When it's over, it's back to me and you against the world. My love is only for you Lena...I promise."

The Prey

In the next few days after Lena and Dante's decision to try their sexual escapade they had actually come to realize that neither really had the nerve to approach a total stranger with such a proposition. No matter how *"sexually free"* people appeared to be these days, the thought of offering one's spouse still felt slightly taboo for them.

Fate however would bump into them and relieve them of the often-arduous task of designing one's own destiny. They would not meet their *"prey"* in cinematic fashion, nor at some romantic place like a park or lake. Instead, Lena finished her spicy chicken sandwich and asked Dante to excuse her form their two-seat booth at Wendy's. It was in this restroom where she would meet the woman who would soon fulfill their fantasies.

Sophia held the door for an elder woman than braced her steps to match the woman's lethargic pace to the counter to order food. After counting at least ten customers she figured she had time to use the restroom quick and probably not lose much time.

Dante glanced up in time to see the nicest backside wrapped in the tightest blue jeans. He couldn't see the face but the figure said it all.

"Damn..." He thought, never once thinking this could be the woman to complete him and Lena's fantasy. No, his thoughts were much more selfish at the moment...

"Oh, I'm sorry," Sophia said, accidentally bumping into the woman who was exiting the bathroom as she was entering.

"It's ok" Lena said, not really wanting to look the woman in the eye; embarrassed that the brush was her fault.

Sophia noticed the woman's earring had fallen and decided to get it to her before using the restroom, why take a chance on the woman leaving before she was finished?

"Excuse me." Sophia said as Lena and Dante were leaving.

"Yes?" Lena asked.

"You dropped your earring Sophia said smiling.

"I knew it" Dante said to himself..." I knew there was no way that face wasn't going to be beautiful."

"Oh, thank you"

"You're welcome, you're very beautiful" Sophia said unable to tame her crush.

"Umm thank you" Lena stuttered sensing attraction in the compliment.

Dante's light bulb went off.

"Excuse me..." He interrupted.

"Please don't be offended, but are you... into women?"

"Lena was shocked at Dante's bluntness. Sophia wasn't.

"I think women are very, very beautiful."

She responded without hesitation and by the second *"very"* Sophia eyes had cut and locked in on Lena's. Lena was hypnotized. Dante was aroused before saying,

"Would you mind if we ate with you..."

Rationale is rarely able to curtail emotional impulses. It seems at times as if the heart controls the mind not the other way around. Had this not been the case, Dante would have been able to control what he was feeling for Sophia. She fit perfectly into his description of beauty. Her style was modest but sexy, her make up accentuated, it didn't overpower, her lips maneuvered seductively in speech and seduction. Sophia's eyes teased; staring hard then quickly darting as if diffident. Her shyness was no intrinsic characteristic however; it was another cultivated machination that appealed to man's primitive attraction to a pure, chaste, untouched woman.

Sophia's allure had Lena briefly questioning her own sexuality.

"So, are you guys like swingers or something?" Sophia asked.

"No...No..." Dante and Lena said simultaneously.

"Why'd you ask that?" Lena asked.

"O, I don't know, it has to take a lot to ask a perfect stranger to have a threesome. I figured maybe you guys had some experience."

They all smiled.

"No, we're not swingers. Actually, this is the first time we've done something this...*crazy* I guess you can say." Dante said before Lena added,

"Yea, we just wanted to try something different. We so happened to have the same fantasy so..."

"So, you decided let's try it; it should keep our sex life interesting." Sophia finished.

"Exactly." Dante said.

"So why me?" Sophia asked.

Lena spoke first.

"Well, it was an easy choice for me. I'm not into women really, I mean, I think they're beautiful creatures but I've never wanted to sleep with one. But, when I saw you I immediately thought, *"If I was into women, this is the type of women I would be with."*

"Well thanks." Sophia responded, reddened by flattery.

"Absolutely, and since we're going to try this it seems like it was meant to be considering the first woman I spotted seems to be a little interested herself..."

Sophia smiled.

"Maybe..." She said playfully.

"So, I'm just curious, whose idea was it? Sophia asked.

"It was all her idea." Dante said smiling.

"Well I'm sure you didn't oppose."

"At first I did. I thought it was some kind of joke or test. But you're right, once I saw she was serious, I was all for it."

"What about now? Do you support her choosing me?"

Sophia was sexy and she knew it. She was very much in control of her sexual output. She wasn't some pretty little naïve girl unaware of the powers of her beauty. No, Sophia was well aware of the power her sexuality and allure had over men. She hated to be judged by mere physical attractiveness alone, but she embraced the advantageous nature of it.

Once again Dante downplayed his excitement.

"Yea, I support her..."

Sophia smiled. Her meal was done but Lena and Dante were most certainly entertaining and she didn't want this to be the last time the three of them hung out.

"We should get together again real soon; go to a *real* restaurant, get to know each other a little better and discuss this *thing* in a little more detail."

Lena and Dante agreed and the three of them parted ways, each entertaining his and her own thoughts on how this would play out.

The Meeting

"I really like this place." Sophia said after fully absorbing the ambiance of the hibachi restaurant Lena and Dante had taken her to.

"I'm just upset I've lived here all my life and had no idea it was here."

Tokyo Diner had become a favorite of Dante and Lena's and they figured it was a nice place to get to know Sophia a little more.

"So, I take it you guys come here often." Sophia said as the waitress left to fetch waters for the threesome.

"Yea...Dante brought me here for our first date, so...I guess you can say it's a little special to us. So, you said you do like it?"

"Oh yea, it's classy, laid back…I do like it actually." Sophia said before picking up her menu.

"So, I'm guessing you two don't play it safe when it comes to the menu…" Sophia smiled mischievously.

"Well, we have been known to experiment a little…" Lena teased.

The threesome blushed with embarrassment but chuckled at the humor and irony of their inside joke.

"Ha ha-ha" Dante said.

"Actually, I play it pretty safe. I try to stick to what I know. Chicken, rice… you know, the usual. Lena on the other hand…"

"So you're the daredevil huh?" Sophia asked Lena.

"I guess I should've known considering this entire thing was your idea…"

Sophia smiled seductively at Lena.

"Yea, I guess you can say that …" Lena said.

"I've always liked to try new things...I just want to live a life rich with experiences, no inhibitions, live and enjoy all life has to offer..."

The stare between Sophia and Lena became instantly intimate.

"Well, thanks to some advice from TLC, I try not to chase waterfalls... I stick to the rivers and the lakes that I'm used to ..." Dante interjected as a hint of jealousy crept into his mind. He had caught the silent exchange between Sophia and Lena. Sometimes a glance says more than words.

"Well, you don't play it too safe..." Sophia said sarcastically.

"I guess you're right." Dante said trying to escape, Sophia's magnetic stare.

After a brief moment of silence, it was silently agreed upon that the three of them were ready for the formalities to end and for the act to begin. The meals were finished in relative silence and rather briskly. The coupled exited together and made plans to meet that weekend at a hotel they all agreed upon. It was official; Lena and Dante were really going to go through with this.

The Act

Lena was nervous...very nervous, and she had no problem admitting this to Dante as they double-checked their belongings.

"That's completely natural. This is a new thing with a perfect stranger. Say what you want about men but I'm a little nervous my damn self."

"Do you love me?" Lena asked.

"Yes I love you Lena, too much."

"I hope so."

Dante and Lena had reserved the room by phone in Sophia's name so when Sophia showed up to the Crown Plaza Hotel all she had to do was grab her key and make herself comfortable in their suite.

Sophia removed her coat and walked towards the bathroom. The shower was nice and it made her smile as she wondered if she and her new friends would make use of it. She smiled at her reflection in the mirror but once again it was one of those smiles that was completely void of humor and merely masked internal pain and confusion. She shook her head in slight disappointment as she thought about how she he had ended up in a hotel room waiting for a strange couple to arrive so she could fulfill their fantasy. This had never been the plan as a child.

Like so many other young women, Sophia's youthful mind had entertained dreams and ambitions of fame and stardom. She wanted to sing, she wanted to model, she wanted to own a fashion line; she wanted to do it all. Then, at eight the molestation began and promiscuity ensued. Then there was the awful rape. O that rape had devastated her and obliterated her love and trust for all men for quite a while. Into the arms of women Sophia had run and into the strip club they had run her. Years of medicating pain and anxiety with drugs followed before she was blessed with a child. The child's existence would inflict a much-needed guilt into her that would give her the embarrassment needed to walk away from the underworld and venture into normalcy. Sophia's daughter passed away but not before changing her life. Somehow, her brief appearance and disappearance was seen as ethereal by Sophia and she found it easier than imagined to accept her angel's departure.

Change was wanted but for Sophia, love was needed for this change to take place. She had been treated rather disrespectfully by men over the years and now she was ready to show just how ready to be a wife she was. Her search often bordered on desperation as she tried her hardest to find the love that through it all she had never given up on.

Sophia's past often interfered with her future however and at the moment, like so many other moments in her life, Sophia was alone. Her loneliness had led her into this crazy act.

"Hey...YOLO!" She said smiling. She had brought a bottle of Patroń, and decided to take a shot...well...two, to settle her nerves and get her in the mood.

"Just have fun..." Sophia said to herself before setting her *Pandora* station to *Melanie Fiona* on her phone and kicking back on the sofa.

"I don't know Dante; don't you feel a little...I don't know...sluttish?" Lena said as they stopped at the entrance of the Crown Plaza.

"Sluttish?" Dante said, teasing Lena.

"You know what I mean."

"No, I know and we both know we're not like this, we don't run around doing this every day. You got an idea...a *great* idea..."

"Shut up." Lena said elbowing Dante in the ribs. He laughed.

"It's ok baby, we're the only ones that know anyway."

"I guess you're right..."

Lena and Dante opened the door to the suite and both of them stopped in their tracks. Sophia was on the bed fully nude. She was gently massaging herself.

"I wanted to make it easy for you guys to get comfortable. Don't think just do. Undress and join me."

It was strange at first but even in the beginning there were flashes of pleasure that made Lena know she would enjoy this just as much as Dante if not more. Dante was already enjoying himself. His lips were on Sophia's and his hands were on Lena's backside. Sophia stroked Dante's manhood and Lena timidly rubbed Sophia's breast. A condom appeared. Arousal heightened, the act began.

Dante started with his fiancé, making love to her in the normal missionary fashion. Had it not been for Sophia's hands all over him and Lena, Dante may have been satisfied with making love to his woman again. Sophia however was not willing to play spectator for very long. She became aggressive; dominant. Rolling Dante over, she straddled him and began to make love to him wildly. The wildness was tamed however when she glanced into Dante's eyes and saw what she thought was much more than lust. His touch became gentle and his sex became love-making. Sophia felt wonderful and now she could see just how wonderful she felt to him. Lena saw this and cut back in.

Dante made love to Lena from behind but never took his eyes off of Sophia who made love to herself with her fingers without ever looking away from Dante. Lena was pleasured but obviously distracted; distracted by the chemistry she had picked up on between Dante and Sophia.

Gently, Dante pushed Lena to the side and crawled towards Sophia. She slid beneath him and Dante began to make love to Sophia like a man in love.

No longer was her mind blinded by the bright lights of fantasy. No, now what hovered low was a dark cloud of reality. The clouds of delusion were fading and the fog of illusion was lifted. The reality that lay before Lena was now frightening. This woman, who was really no more than a stranger, was having an orgasm. Sophia's body and soul were momentarily one with her fiancé's. Jealous rage consumed her and her arousal quickly subsided. She was ready for this to be over.

Lena was now questioning why she had suggested this. She was upset but how mad could she be? She brought it up. Lena's eyes fought back tears as she watched Dante make love to Sophia just as passionately as he had done with her so many times.

Dante and Sophia had gotten so lost in each other that neither noticed that Lena was no longer participating. Slowly Lena crawled out of the bed. After untangling her panties from Sophia's, she slid them on and reached under the bed for her bra. As she did Sophia's moaning grew louder and she began to climax again. Dante sat back with an egoistic smile on his face as he too was in bliss after bringing Sophia to another orgasm. It was at this point that he glanced to his side and caught the liquid stare of Lena who was finally dressed. Lena shook her head and walked towards the door.

"Wait...where you goin?"

Lena smiled one of the smiles that merely disguise a frown.

"Nice meeting you." She said to Sophia.

"Love you." She mouthed to Dante before walking out.

"Lena!" Dante called out but Sophia quickly placed her finger on Dante's lips.

"Let her go...we still have the moment..."

Sophia moved her finger and bit down on Dante's bottom lip nearly drawing blood. Slowly she regained her rhythm and began her dance again. Again, Lena had faded from Dante's memory.

Lena's insecurity had only made Sophia more confident. Before Lena's abrupt departure Sophia hadn't felt as if she could have Dante alone but now she did. Sophia's forlorn heart wanted to feel special. She wanted to feel the love Lena felt and she would try her hardest to make Dante fall in love. Her moaning became a sonnet, her riding became a dance; her stream became a river and her sighs became cries. She scratched red streams of passion down his back and arms destined to leave her mark. Satisfied that she had done so physically and mentally, she rode the waves of orgasm then collapsed onto Dante's chest. Dante knew he should leave...right then...he should leave and go after his fiancé...but he didn't.

Sophia nestled closely to Dante's heaving chest, wrapping her arms comfortably around his warm torso. His ripped abdomen was still flexing thanks to his sexual workout and Sophia felt that even in exhaustion he looked gorgeous. If Adonis was the pinnacle of male beauty than Dante was the almond version and now in this moment of beautiful silence, he was all hers. She would not worry herself with how long this moment would last; she would only enjoy the fact that she was living in it.

The silence was slightly uncomfortable for Dante however. What was he supposed to do or say now to his new paramour? Sophia was still a stranger. They hadn't had much of a conversation before this took place. Then there was the dread of what Lena must have been thinking; what she must have been feeling.

The blissful clouds of fantasy were again dissipating, only to be replaced by an overcast of gray reality clouds. This may be the last time Dante and Sophia would see each other and experience the euphoric ecstasy of sexual freedom unencumbered by societal norms. It was now time to return to the normalcy of monogamy, a normalcy that would now inevitably seem mundane in contrast to the titillating debauchery they had just experienced.

For Sophia, the feelings were more possessive, more attached. It's easier to be a guest than a host; to enter than to permit entrance. To accept an invitation to a sacred temple pales in comparison to inviting a stranger into one. No matter how much times change it seems women still cling to a lover more than a man and Sophia, though she thought she would be stronger, was falling victim to this inability to write sex off as just sex. In her eyes, the act was still sacred and the person she enjoyed it with just as much so. There was no way she would allow this to be the last time she made love to Dante. In a time of hyper masculinity and selfishness, men seemed to be so out of tune with their inner artist, with their poetic nature and sensual side. This, in Sophia's eyes, had men out of tune with the makeup of a woman and how to truly be great lovers. An orgasm seemed to be hard to come by nowadays and now that Dante had guided her to not one but three, she was enamored.

After the cinematic break from her last lover, Sophia's sex life had been reduced to masturbation and synthetic stimulation. She had tried watching pornography but in her eyes, it was too animalistic. There was no passion just what resembled wild animals copulating and men who could care less about what the woman was feeling. At times it appeared degrading and she realized it usually turned her off more than on. Toys were fine until those brief moments of realization kicked in and she would glimpse at her reflection in the mirror. She felt she looked so desperate, weird even, with these battery charged rubber and plastic objects that were supposed to serve as replacements for the real thing. Sometimes a bit of shame would flush through her. Her favorite lover now was merely her manicured fingers and vivid imagination.

Now that Sophia had experienced the intense passion of a man again, she was addicted. Something about the climactic pleasure was driving Sophia to the cliffs of insanity. The passion was building, she was climbing, and the climax had left her staring over the edge into a dark canyon of irrationality. It was becoming impossible for the screams of rationale to talk her out of jumping. Already at the point of no return, her mind and emotions took a plunge into that abyss of crazed infatuation. Sophia was now falling into that bottomless pit of darkness known as love where few

hearts make it out of.

The Aftermath

Dante walked slowly to the door. He felt like a sheep being led to a slaughter. He knew an explosive argument was inevitable.

"After seeing how I left, seeing how I felt, you still decided to stay the night with her?"

Dante was shaking his head in disappointment. How did he let Sophia seduce him into staying with her all night? No matter how good she was, how beautiful she was, or how new the feeling was, his loyalty was to Lena and he should have stopped as soon as Lena left. Instead, he allowed his hormones to navigate his course.

"Lena, I'm sorry baby, I fell asleep."

"I left at 10:00 Dante... 10 o' clock!" It's now 10:00am; you stayed with her another 12 hours! Was it that good?"

"C'mon Lena Don't do that to me..."

"Don't do what to you, tell you the truth."

"It was your idea in the first place." Dante reasoned in his own defense.

"Lena was briefly silenced, it was her idea, and what a stupid one. What made her believe she could share the man she loved and cherished? As far as she knew Dante had never cheated and now she had given him permission to sleep with another woman. She was so angry with herself but this didn't excuse Dante staying out all night with this stranger.

"Listen, listen, Lena... I made a mistake and I'm sorry" ... This whole thing was a mistake. He added hoping to clandestinely shift some of the blame. He always had to remind Lena that this was all her idea.

"Let's just put it behind us now, please. We still have a wedding to plan, children to make, and a home to build. I got caught up in the moment but Lena, you have my heart. I'm not leaving you and I'm willing to fight hard as hell for you not to leave me!

"Look" Dante said grabbing Lena's shoulder to settle her nervous shaking...

"We tried something. It didn't go right. I let it go too far. I should've stopped when you stopped. I didn't and I'm sorry for that. Can we just move on? I'm telling you I want you! Believe that, know that, and trust that! Cause I mean it!"

Dante forced Lena to stare directly into his eyes.

"Ok?"

After some hesitation, Lena nodded yes. The surrender was actually a relief for Lena who exhaled a heavy load of resentment. What could she do, it was what it was. She was at blame for introducing the idea in the first place.

After a few weeks, things returned to normal and though they hadn't forgotten what had happened, they had found a way to put it behind them. One of the things they had done to do so was fishing. They would get into fishing and get away together every Sunday. Lena could read and Dante could busy himself with the oft-tedious task of catching fish.

It was one of their routine outings when Sophia showed up at their home.

"Hey babe, let's go! The earlier the better."

"I'm coming, I'm coming." Lena shouted from their bedroom as she touched up her face in the vanity mirror.

Dante Walked outside to load the car. As he tried to remain focused on fish, and bait, and location, and technique a woman who had been jogging nearby stopped and called his name.

"Dante?" The woman asked. She wanted to be sure she wasn't mistaking the man for someone else.

Dante recognized the woman immediately and his heart dropped. Instinctively his head spun towards the house to make sure Lena wasn't looking out of any windows.

"Sophia what are you doing here?"

"I was just taking a jog that's all."

"Stop with the bullshit you don't even live in this neighborhood."

"Dante why are you ignoring me like this?"

"Sophia, because I can't..."

"Yes you can. And you want to. Sophia glanced over in time to see Lena walking out of the house. She quickly handed Dante a card.

"Call me!" She said before putting on her earphones and jogging away.

"What are you looking at?" Lena said as she made her way to the car.

"And who was that?"

"Hah, umm I don't know, some woman. I wasn't looking."

"Ahh, hah, some woman…" Lena said skeptically.

"And you were looking; you almost broke your neck."

That close call was not enough to keep Dante from calling Sophia. Just seeing her again had brought back so many memories. He couldn't fight the urge this time. And this time, he gave into temptation and began having an affair with Sophia.

The Affair

Sophia and Dante began seeing each other as much as often. For Dante, this was strenuous because the more time he spent with Sophia the more time she demanded and it was something he no longer had much of to spare. Being engaged to Lena and still trying to move forward with their plans of unification while at the same time entertaining Sophia's dreams to do the same thing were slowly exhausting him.

No matter how exhausting he couldn't find his way out of the maze he was now in. Sophia was very deep and her love was deeper. It was an ocean that Dante submerged himself in every chance he could. Sophia was a mystery that piqued his curiosity and the regret he often felt was simply not enough to stop him from entertaining this curiousness.

Besides the mystery was the reality. Sophia's soul had been tortured thus far in life. Abused by men and misused by life, her heart was now a shadow of its once radiant self. She had become very numb. Dante soon found himself wanting to help Sophia; wanting to fix her.

In a fight, Sophia had told Dante,

"You don't really know me."

"I beg to differ." He said, not at all fazed by her warning.

"Why is that?" Sophia had asked, slightly confused by Dante's response.

"To say I don't know you is to say I don't know myself. We're one in the same."

"How do you figure?" Sophia asked.

"How do you figure we're not?" Dante shot right back.

Not in the mood to play his game, Sophia said, *"I have a past."* very flatly.

Just as calm and even-toned, Dante replied.

"And so do I. Every rose has its thorns, and he who wants a rose must respect the thorns. One of the most admired flowers can also be one of the most painful...like love...Am I perfect? No, I'm cheating on my fiancé right now..."

The reality of his words stung but Sophia didn't interrupt.

"I'm human too is what I'm saying. If I was in complete control I wouldn't have let this get this far; not because I don't like it but because it's wrong."

And even after admitting it was wrong, Dante made love to Sophia again.

When the two were alone, Sophia felt complete. Dante was now her world and she hated that his love had come at another woman's cost but she couldn't let it go. And even if they were discovered and she was labeled a home wrecker, well, Sophia was fine with that, she had been called worse. And that was a very small price to pay for a lifetime of happiness with such an incredible man.

There were plenty of times where Dante had tried to walk away but often realized he had already gone too far. Sophia was at the point now where any separation would be unbearable. He was now something she would fight for and as crazy as it may have sounded, she now felt Dante was partly hers.

If there was an area in which Lena lacked, she would fill that void. So, Sophia listened closely to Dante's every complaint. If Lena did something wrong, she would do it right. If Lena hadn't exposed him to something yet, she would. He loved to read so she became a writer. Her natural gift for writing was a serendipitous discovery that had begun as nothing more than a ploy to please Dante. It was this power in Dante that Sophia was addicted to; his ability to pull the best out of her.

This tug-a-war love affair would go on for weeks. Dante would always make Sophia believe he would be hers but would always end up letting her down. She knew that it wasn't that he didn't love her; it was that he still owed Lena and felt obligated to her. Selfishly, Sophia no longer cared at what expense Dante's love came and she began to intentionally leave clues, praying Lena would discover the illicit affair and she could finally have Dante to herself.

Dante's mind became dizzy in those few weeks of infidelity. He was under Sophia's spell. He knew it but couldn't fight it. She was slowly making him lose sight of the love he had found in Lena and Lena noticed this more than anyone.

Dante and Lena had been together for so long that any slight nuance in his behavior was easy to notice. Dante had become absent and a whole lot less affectionate. Any affection he did show felt forced and/or premeditated. Something had come between her and her man but Lena was willing to fight to save their relationship.

Sophia had the same thought in mind and before he knew it, Dante was constantly fighting Lena's allegations, and Sophia's ploys to destroy what was left of his relationship. Sophia was trying everything now from perfuming his clothes to showing up unexpectedly at his job.

"Sophia, you can't just be showing up at my job like this." Dante said as he put the flowers down in the backseat of Sophia's Camry.

"And why would you have the flowers delivered? You could've just given them to me this weekend."

"Well I didn't feel like waiting to the weekend and I thought you may appreciate it. Sorry,

I won't do anything nice anymore. I'll continue to hide and be available to you only when you want to see me."

"C'mon Sophia, don't do that."

"Do what Dante? It's the truth. You want to see me when you want to see me, what about when I get the urge to see you? Like today, I thought about you, so I got you some flowers to show you and I actually did hand deliver them I just asked your partner to give them to you because I knew you wouldn't want me coming in there. So actually, I was thinking, and I was mindful of your situation but why don't you ever consider or care for how I may feel. Dante, do you have any idea how I feel at night when you're not with me? To know that you're holding her, caressing her, telling her you love her; do you have any idea how it feels to love someone but have to *hope* they answer your calls, well your *texts* because you're not *allowed* to call? You don't! You text, I text right back and if you call I come running. And now, I can't even do things to show my affection for you? Do you know you told me you love me Dante?"

"Yes Sophia, of course I know what I told you."

"Do you know what that means? And not just what it means but what it means to a person who has been so deprived of it. Do you know you can hurt people Dante? I've been hurt, by men who said they loved me but they had an ulterior motive. You said you were different, but are you...really?"

"Of course I am Sophia, you know I am..."

"No I thought you were, but what I'm starting to realize is you have the same ulterior motive. Sex is the ultimate agenda; you're just clever enough to mask your intentions."

"No I'm not..."

"Yes you are Dante. You use me as an emotional and sexual escape from Lena. The sad part is I can see how this ends. Soon you'll get tired of my sex, as all men do with women, but unlike Lena, there will be nothing to keep you connected to me. No children, no engagement. You know I'll be hurt, but you'll reason that I'll get over it in time and slowly you'll push me out of your mind. I know how this story plays out; I've seen the movie a thousand times."

Guilt was killing Dante. He really did love Sophia, and he now realized he had let this go on to the point that there was no way this would end on a good note. Someone was going to get hurt, very badly.

"Listen, Sophia, I don't just tell you I love you for sex, or, just for the sake of saying it..."

"Well why do you say it?"

"Because, I mean it."

"Prove it." Sophia said stubbornly. She was slowly growing tired of Dante's inability to make up his mind. Making up one's mind is not the hard part however, making up one's heart was a lot more difficult. The mind submissively follows the convictions of the heart.

"How?"

"Follow your heart."

"I did, and it got me in this mess."

"Mess, wow, just last night it was beauty, now it's a mess?"

"That's not what I mean…"

"That's what you said."

"Stop! Sophia, I'm not perfect and obviously I'm not heartless. If I was heartless I would have done the right thing and stopped this affair, admitted it to my fiancé, and begin work on making things right if she was willing to. I don't want to hurt you or her."

"Well soon Dante, you're not going to have a choice, you're gonna have to make a decision and one of us is gonna have to deal with the pain of loss…"

"Or we can all end up dealing with loss…"

Sophia went silent. She could only push so much. In the end, she didn't want to lose Dante or do anything to make him contemplate leaving her. No matter how much she appeared to be making an ultimatum, she knew it was weightless. It was her attempt to appear in control of a situation she realized she wasn't. She wouldn't have ever left Dante, he would have to leave her, and even that would be hard.

"Look Sophia, I'm trying to figure this out and if you want me to leave you alone to do it I will…"

That was exactly what Sophia *didn't* want to hear. Knowing her bluff had been called and she had been defeated, Sophia's shoulders dropped along with her head. Where was her dignity going? She asked herself as she mumbled,

"No, that's not what I want…"

"It's enough that you show up at my house, at… but now you're compromising my livelihood.

This is how I survive, how I feed myself and my family. You're taking this too far. Sophia, this has to end; for the sake of everyone involved."

"How am I taking this too far? Dante maybe you should've thought about that before you agreed to this. I'm not just some worthless object you can throw away whenever you're done. What, now that I satisfied your lust for something you were missing at home, you're ready to get rid of me? It doesn't work like that Dante."

"That's exactly how it works Sophia. We agreed to a fling, not a relationship."

"You labeled it a fling, I just agreed to wanting to see you again."

"Whatever the case, this situation was supposed to be a no-strings affair..."

"Why are you being so mean to me right now..."

A pang of guilt shot through Dante's heart as tears began to well up in Sophia's eyes.

"I'm sorry..."

"Dante, you make love to me like I'm your wife, is it my fault you get caught up in the passion? I mean, I can't help that my feelings for you have grown."

"Sophia you're right... I know... and I'm sorry. That's not what I wanted to happen."

"Well that's what happened and I know I can't have you exclusively but you can't just ditch me like this Dante, you just can't do that... Like, what did I do?"

"Sophia, it's not what you did...I mean showing up at my place was definitely not cool but that's not it, it's not something you did, it's the fact that I'm engaged."

"I understand that and I'm fine with it."

"You're fine with knowing I have a fiancé, soon a wife, and the fact that there may be no chance of a future with us?"

"Yes."

"C'mon Sophia..."

"No, I'm serious, I really love you Dante and I'd rather have some of you then none of you, since I can't have all of you."

Dante paused. Sophia's last statement made him realize just how infatuated Sophia had become. Dante labeled it infatuation because the love Sophia was proclaiming was not a love that was exclusive for him. This was a void in her soul that she was trying to fill and he just so happened to fit. That was all he could reason as he tried to wrap his mind around Sophia's desperation.

"Sophia C'mon, you have to have more pride in yourself than that, you know, some dignity. You're telling me your fine with just being my thing on the side..."

"No, that's what you're saying. I'm saying I'll wait, six months, a year, whatever it takes to make you realize that you should be with me. I'm not fine with being second, but I'm fine with waiting my turn to be first."

Dante was going to respond, but noticed his lunch break was over.

"We'll finish this later."

"I hope so." Sophia said.

Dante got up to leave and Sophia was going to let him, but she couldn't. She never could.

"Are you really that mad at me? No kiss?"

Dante shook his head and smiled at the irony. Sophia felt Dante was obligated to treat her exactly as he would Lena. She wasn't wrong for this; he had told her he loved her.

"Of course." Dante said before leaning over to extend a kiss.

"So I'll see you later than?" Sophia asked.

"Yes."

The Discovery

Lena double-checked her appearance in the driver side window of her car. It had been a while since she had shown up to Dante's job unexpected but she knew it was one of the sacrifices she would have to make to get her man's full attention again. They hadn't even as much as spoken about the wedding after their episode with Sophia and Lena was starting to worry Dante may have been getting cold feet.

Lena reached into the backseat and grabbed the single rose and card she bought him. In the passenger seat was a platter of seafood for his lunch. Gathering everything she had brought Dante, Lena checked her watch...

"Dang!" She mumbled. Her tucked lips were clenching on the card she now held with her mouth. She was late and wouldn't be able to spend lunch with Dante like she had planned. Still, she hustled her way into the building in case Dante was still on his lunch.

Once inside one of Dante's co-workers, knowing who Lena was, greeted her than offered to get him for her. He had already returned to work. As he was turning on his heels the sight of the rose finally processed and Julius smiled and said,

"Oh, forgot one huh? Dante must be a really good dude, you came all the way back to bring him one rose...how sweet."

Lena looked confused and Julius realized immediately that he had made a mistake. Nervousness now shook his heart and beads of sweat began to accumulate on his brow. How would he get out of this? Not only was Lena now flaming with rage, Dante would be to once he found out who was responsible for his fiancé discovering his affair.

"What are you talking about?" Was all Lena could come up with, although she was very aware of what the man was saying. Someone had already brought Dante flowers and the thought of who it may have been was destroying Lena inside.

"Nuh...nothing..."

"No, don't stutter and don't get amnesia all of a sudden, you were just so articulate and charming. Maybe the fact that you're about to lie to me is causing some difficulty inside..."

"Look...I don't know, who, what...look I don't know anything, all I know is Dante came from break with some flowers, that's it. I just assumed they were from you."

"And now you realize they weren't and that you messed up."

Julius was silent. He knew it was best to quit while he was ahead and not say anything else that may get him into deeper waters.

"What did she look like?"

Julius just ignored her and led the way to where Dante was working. He asked Lena to hold on as he summoned Dante.

Dante smiled when Julius called his name but when he saw the look on Julius's pale face, he knew something was wrong.

"Wassup bro, you look like you saw a ghost."

"Not a ghost...the devil himself." Julius thought as he hung his head in shame.

"I messed up man. I had no idea someone else brought you flowers...your fiancé came in and I mentioned them..."

"And now I want to know who the hell is bringing my man flowers to his job?" Lena interjected furiously.

Dante's eyes shot to Lena's they were bloodshot; then to Julius's, they were guilt-ridden; then to the flowers...they spoke without speaking.

"Excuse us." Dante said to Julius.

"My bad man..."

"Just go, it's cool." Dante said. No matter how upset he wanted to be with Julius he knew he couldn't. His infidelity had gotten him into this; Julius's big mouth was just the conduit through which Karma manifested itself.

"Lena..."

"WHO?"

"Listen..."

"WHO?"

Everything inside of Dante was saying lie; make up a story; it could've been anyone; compliments of the company; anything... He couldn't however manufacture a satisfactorily lie in the brief millisecond in which Lena would be expecting a reply. So, he spewed the truth...some of it.

"Listen Lena, Sophia found me somehow. She found out where I worked and she wanted to drop some flowers off. Probably not smart but she actually mentioned you and said she was just thinking about us and wanted to express it. I mean, it is flowers, and I am a man, so maybe they were meant more for..."

"Don't play with me Dante, are you seeing this woman?"

"No."

"Let me see your phone."

"My phone?"

"Yes, *your phone*, let me see it."

Dante complied. He had long deleted any messages that had been exchanged between him and Sophia.

After a brief search that produced zero evidence, Lena gave Dante his phone back.

"Why is she bringing you flowers Dante? Why is she even still around?"

Dante answered these questions and what seemed to be a hundred more by the night's end.

By the next morning the suspicion had grown into conviction. There was no way that woman just showed up without some prior communication with Dante. If it was one thing Lena knew, men will often try to play the *Stalker Card* when caught cheating; that being, labeling the mistress a stalker to relieve themselves of any guilt. True, some women did get *stalkerish*, but only after their feelings have been somehow toyed with.

Lena was right, as she followed Dante that next week she would discover that not only was he still seeing Sophia, but he was now the pursuer. Once that week he had gone shopping at Macy's for her. Twice he had gotten her flowers. He had taken her to dinner, and even managed to attend a carnival in a town twenty minutes from where they lived.

Lena found two things odd; one was how fast Dante would get to Sophia, it wasn't as if they spent much time apart, the other was how oblivious he was to her following him. His thoughts in that period were too consumed with Sophia and his illicit affair with her.

What was killing her inside was how genuinely happy appeared to be with Sophia. This is what hurt the most. It made her question herself, even though she knew she had no reason to. And now watching her man spend time, blissfully, with another woman was killing her. And even after being confronted with pictures and evidence, Dante went back to Sophia the very next week. Lena could see it in Dante's eyes, he was in love. Of course she knew the look because she had melted in its flattery early in their relationship as well. It was a look he held only for her until they met Sophia. No, Lena would not lose her man without a fight. She had already lost his love; she could feel and see that. But now, with Sophia in the way they would never be able to regain that love. This thought was driving Lena mad. Eventually, it would drive her to murder.

The End

As Lena made her way towards the door, drenched in rain, and soaked in pain, a terror began to rise in her chest as she realized she was afraid of the monster this situation had created. She had never been a violent soul; competitive but not combative. Violence in movies bothered her; let alone real-life violence. Yet here she was, gun in hand, vendetta in mind, and prepared to take the life of the woman that had stolen her love away.

Lena knew the two were here alone in this Bungalow as she had followed Dante every day for the past week. She had taken a leave of absence from work and had unfortunately, confirmed what she knew to be true. Dante had continued seeing Sophia. They were having an affair.

Lena raised her hand to knock on the door but apprehension stopped her from knocking. A myriad of emotions dizzied Lena's confused mind. She feared embarrassment, humiliation, degradation; she feared many things but not enough to not go through with this. She had been destroyed by pain and it was time for someone else to experience it.

A hesitant knock was followed by three booming ones that startled the illicit lovers inside. Panic overtook Sophia and Dante immediately. No one was supposed to know they were here so who could be knocking of this hour? They both began suffering from the same dreadful thought; it was Lena at the door. She was scorned and broken hearted and she probably had hate in her heart and revenge in her eyes.

Sophia sat up in bed and pulled the sheets closely to her body.

"Put your robe on." Dante whispered as he crept through the house to the window in order to get a good look at their visitor. Because of the rain, darkness, and angle of the window, Dante was unable to see who it actually was. He could see that the person was small in stature; most likely a woman, and most likely Lena.   His   heart fluttered and Sophia sensed the paranoia.

"Is it her?" Sophia asked.

"I think so."

"What are you gonna do?"

"You have to hide."

"Hide" Sophia questioned upset.

"I'm not some teenage girl sneaking in to your mom's house. I'm not hiding…"

"Sophia, not now!"

"No, Dante, I'm tired of hiding, it's time for you to be a man and tell her how you feel about me."

"Not now; not like this. It would hurt her too much."

Again there was a loud thud at the door followed by a shock to Dante's heart.

"What about me Dante. Why are you always pushing my feelings aside to protect hers? Why do you care more about how she feels then I do? I love you too Dante... Why do you do this to me? You get me all excited, like you love me and really wanna be with me but..."

Dante fell silent. He had no rebuttal. He had allowed Sophia to fall in love and now he was paying for it double-fold. His fiancé was at the door in pain and Sophia was now in tears as well.

Again, there was a knock but this time it was followed by a voice ordering Dante to open the door. If there was any doubt left it was gone now; that was most definitely Lena at the door.

Dante took a deep breath and proceeded to the door. He looked back at Sophia once more before turning the knob. She simply shook her head no and said,

"I'm not hiding."

Dante was no longer going to fight it. Sophia was right. He had to face Lena. He had to tell her the truth. He had to tell her what he felt for Sophia but once he opened the door. He couldn't.

Lena's mascara had trailed below her cheek, adding emphasis to her streams of tears. She was hurt, beyond repair, and the pain and shame it caused Dante was unbearable. There was no way he could hurt her. They had shared so much of life together. They had so many memories, and now he was reminded of this.

"Where is she?" Lena asked.

"Lena, Listen…" As Dante tried to place his hands on Lena's shoulder to calm her, Sophia called out…

"Baby who is it? Come back to bed." It was intentional; she was tired of hiding and playing this game. If Dante wasn't going to tell Lena he loved her, she would! Dante dropped his head and shook it as he anticipated what was next. He would only have a second to ponder Lena's next move. She stepped back and kicked as hard as she could at the door. Her eyes were like those of a raging bull's and for the first time ever. Dante was genuinely afraid of Lena.

In that split second of heightened fear, Dante missed the shiny metallic object in Lena's hand but it was clearly visible now. Sophia was screaming, squirming around in the bed, with her hands in front of her, she plead with Lena not to kill her; Dante began to do the same.

"Lena...Lena...take it easy...Please... think about what you're doing..."

Lena was dead silent. She hadn't responded at all to what Dante was saying, nor to Sophia's pleads; only the voice of vengeance telling her she would never be satisfied until she avenged her honor.

"Lena...you can't just kill somebody...it won't end here Lena, think...it ends in a courtroom Lena, with you going to prison forever. Nobody's worth that...not even me."

His words fell on deaf ears. Dante could see that Lena had blocked out the world and all she could see was Sophia...Dying.

"Lena No!" Dante said as he watched, Lena's fingers gripping tighter around the trigger.

Dante quickly stepped in front of the gun.

"Why are you protecting her Dante? Why are you protecting *HER*!?"

"Lena, I'm protecting you! You don't have to do this. I see how hurt you are and that's enough. You don't have to go any further."

Dante looked back at Sophia.

"It's over Sophia. Do you see what this is causing us all? I don't care what happened or how it happened it has to stop." Sophia dropped her head knowingly. No matter what she felt, Dante was right. Sophia was a woman and she now felt this woman's pain.

"Lena, give me the gun."

"Ok." Lena said. Her tensed muscles relaxed and she surrendered the weapon to Dante.

"It's gonna be..."

Before Dante could say *"ok"* There was a loud blast. Dante stared deep into Lena's eyes and whispered..."

"Sorry..."

A gush of blood spewed from his mouth and he swooned to the floor. Sophia screamed. She had covered her mouth but the cries were far from muffled. Lena drifted back in freight and disbelief. Her eyes were wide with shock. Her mouth too was wide open but not a sound escaped her lips. Terrified, her trembling fingers finally released the gun and it fell to the floor.

Sophia flew off the bed and pressed as hard as she could at the wound. It was spilling blood too quickly for her hands to cover. She began speaking to Dante calmly and Lena watched in silence from the shadows. She was paralyzed by shock.

Holding his limp body in her arms, Sophia felt guilt. Yet staring over at the woman that had shot him, she felt rage. Dante had brought Sophia back to life; he had stitched her torn heart. He made her dream again and gave her hope. He gave her strength, taught her and most importantly, he had loved her. She would never forgive herself knowing she could have prevented this horrible accident.

The guilt doubled as Sophia stared into the dimming eyes of the man she felt was her only true lover. The sirens sounded too far away to save him. She wanted to leave but hope made her stay. Hope that Dante wouldn't die here like this. He didn't deserve it. Bullets, blood, and the stench of death; it wasn't supposed to be like this. She wasn't even supposed to love him.

Dante choked on a clot of blood and continued to grimace in pain. He tried to speak but couldn't. Instead, that was how he died, struggling to find the right words to explain how he had loved them both no matter how wrong or right, and how he had only wanted to make them both feel special.

Jaded

The heart is not a bone
It can't be broken or crushed
Nor shattered for that matter
So the matter is the matter
Cannot calcify or ossify
Can't stop itself from healing
So in turn cannot stop itself
From feeling what it's feeling...
Heartache is a pain where once is too much
So if we really had a choice
I think once would be enough
But that's never the case...
We do build great fortresses of brick and mortar
Drawbridges, hidden quarters
Moats with alligators in pits of water
But, conquerors are clever
Scientist create earthquakes
Walls fall, the earth shakes
You're as naked as your birth date
Then, no matter how
Jaded or, Faded or, Tainted
You're persuaded by persuasions
To just be courageous
The tragedy's not the pain
It's to no longer feel it
And though that time inflicted wounds
Know in time,
Time will heal it

-Saleem Little